Ahoy, Julian! This be for you.

R.G.G.

⚓

For my son, Jarrod.

B.A.

Text Copyright © 2013 Rhonda Gowler Greene • Illustration Copyright © 2013 Brian Ajhar

Sleeping Bear Press™ • 315 E. Eisenhower Parkway, Suite 200 • Ann Arbor, MI 48108 • www.sleepingbearpress.com

Printed and bound in the United States.

10 9 8 7 6 5 4 3 2 1

Library of Congress Cataloging-in-Publication Data
Greene, Rhonda Gowler.
No pirates allowed! said Library Lou / written by Rhonda Gowler Greene ; illustrated by Brian Ajhar.
p. cm.
Summary: Big Pirate Pete's treasure map has led him to Seabreezy Library, where Library Lou must convince him that the true treasure is the books.
ISBN 978-1-58536-796-2
[1. Stories in rhyme. 2. Libraries—Fiction. 3. Books and reading—Fiction. 4. Pirates—Fiction. 5. Buried treasure—Fiction.] I. Ajhar, Brian, ill. II. Title.
PZ8.3.G824No 2013   [E]—dc23
2012033685

NO PIRATES ALLOWED!

Said Library Lou

By Rhonda Gowler Greene

Illustrated by Brian Ajhar

At Seabreezy Library, things were just right.
Book lovers were cozy. The sky was blue-bright
when—Shiver me timbers!—through Seabreezy's door
stormed Big Pirate Pete and his parrot, Igor!

"Whar be the treasure?! X marks this spot!
We'll dig up the loot an' steal all that ye've got!"

Chills ran down spines as those readers all shook.
They hid behind bookshelves, but ventured a look.
And what was that odor? Disgusting! Phhhew!
But no one at Seabreezy knew what to do.

Except...
Library Lou who dashed over to see
what all the unruly commotion could be.
"May I help you?" Lou asked with a pinch of a frown.
"This is a library.
Shhh! Quiet down!"

"ARRGH!"

Big Pete thundered.
   "Don't waste me day!
Walk the plank, saucy lass, or show me the way!"

At Seabreezy then, you could hear a pin drop.
All that tough, ruffian talk and squawk stopped
   for Library Lou looked Pete right in the eye
as Pete stood his ground with a snarl. Oh, my!

Minute by minute, their tempers both flared
as they stood head to head and doggedly dared!

"Unless you be quiet...and listen up too...

NO PIRATES ALLOWED!"

said Library Lou.

SQUAWK! Igor squawked with a blow-me-down glare.
Then Library Lou boldly added—**"So there!"**

ARRGH!

"Now—
where is the treasure map?" Lou asked.
        "...ahhh, yes."

"The treasure is here," she said. "Just as I guessed."

"I'll help you find it. But first I must ask
        of you and your matey a wee smallish task—
Go home. Take a bath. Change your underwear too.
        Then come back tomorrow," said Library Lou.

ARRGH!

A landlubber tellin' Big Pete what to *do*?!
But—she said thar be treasure. Sink me! 'Tis true!

So...

that night Pete scrubbed thirteen layers of dirt
and decided clean underwear (*sniff!*) couldn't hurt.
Squawking Igor got a good scrubbin' too!
Swwwish through the sea sailed their funky P.U.

Then later they dreamed ...
of a treasure or two.

SQUAWK-AW-AWK!

The next day they burst through that library door
with a fresh, soapy scent, but—as **LOUD** as before!

"Mateys! Your manners!" said Library Lou
"Now, come. Follow me.
We have much work to do."

Aye!

Big Pete grabbed his picks and his ax and his shovel.
But Library Lou said, "Don't go to the trouble."
"But, Lassie! The loot!"
Lou said, "Not yet . . .

First—
say **Ahoy** to these letters!
This fine alphabet!"

"Letters?" Pete scowled. "Thar be more than **X**?"
Lou spread them all out.
Big Pete looked perplexed.
"Blimey!" cried Big Pete. "A code! Of old!
A secret one—Aye!—to find the sweet gold!"

Library Lou grinned a witty-wise grin.
  "Brilliant!" she cried. "Now time to begin!"
"Here they are. All of them. Pleased to meet you.
  Isn't this fun?!" said Library Lou.

"Fun?" Big Pete sneered. "It be torture no less!
  Me'd rather be kissin' a fat treasure chest!"

So many letters! Big Pete got confused!

W's? H's? S's? And Q's?

Some she called vowels—
  A's, E's, I's, O's, and U's?

Soon Lou took some letters and mixed them about.
"Look!" exclaimed Lou. "*Words* to sound out!
Now here is a stack you may take home with you.
Then come back tomorrow," said Library Lou.

Up on the poop deck, Pete practiced that night.
He practiced each word till he got each word right.
"Igor," he bragged, "we'll hold riches untold!
'Cause us? We be hard-workin' gluttons fer gold!"

Yes, day after day after day, he went back.
And night after night, Lou piled high a new stack.

Soon...
Big Pete was reading not small words, but **BIG**—

swashbucklin'

...buccaneer

...thingamajig.

But Pete got impatient. He'd worked day and night
and *still* not a trinket or treasure in sight!

One day he barked at Lou,

"Do what ye told!
Ye said ye'd be helpin' me find that sweet gold!"

"Correct!" answered Lou. "In a book, there's a clue.
I've given my help. It's now...
up to you."

Pete stared at those books lined up shelf... after shelf!
A code? A clue?

ARRGH! "Me find 'em me-self!"

Maybe, just maybe, the code be in rhyme.
He *loved* Mother Goose. Dr. Seuss—how sublime!
They tickled his fancy, but—
no secret code.

Avast! Easy readers!
He snatched *Frog and Toad*.

Day after day after day, he went back.
And night after night, he piled high a new stack.
He found books called classics, great tales of the sea.
"Blimey!" cried Big Pete. "Thar's whar the clue be!

Treasure Island…Me like it!" But—
no clue to be found.

Stumped, Big Pete scoured each shelf, up and down.

Gangway! The *non*-fiction!
     Thar's whar she be!
Soon, luscious loot! Fancy-free on the sea!

Those factual books, Big Pete came to love.
     He read about things that he'd never heard of—
stink bugs… and baseball… and surfing… and Mars…
     dinosaurs, mummies, electric guitars!

Pete's picks and his ax and his shovel got… dusty.
     At piratey ways, Big Pete got a might… rusty.

Now—
　　Pete wasn't a pirate just dreaming of loot,
　　　　but a *reader* he was, and a good one to boot!
　　When one book was finished, yes, when one was done,
　　　　Pete picked up another. Oh, reading was— fun!

He read and he read and he read and he read!
Then suddenly one night, Pete popped up in bed.

The next day...

at Seabreezy Library, things were just right.
Book lovers were cozy. The sky was blue-bright
when Big Pete and Igor tiptoed through the door (*shhh...*)
and spied Library Lou in aisle four hundred four.

They both gave her hugs. Each, a kiss too.
"We've come to thank ye, Miss Library Lou!
'Cause of ye, now we know—
books be the treasure!"
"Shucks," whispered Lou.

"It's been my pleasure."

Now—
Library Lou, with a smile, big and proud,
is hanging a sign that says—

PIRATES...**ALLOWED.**